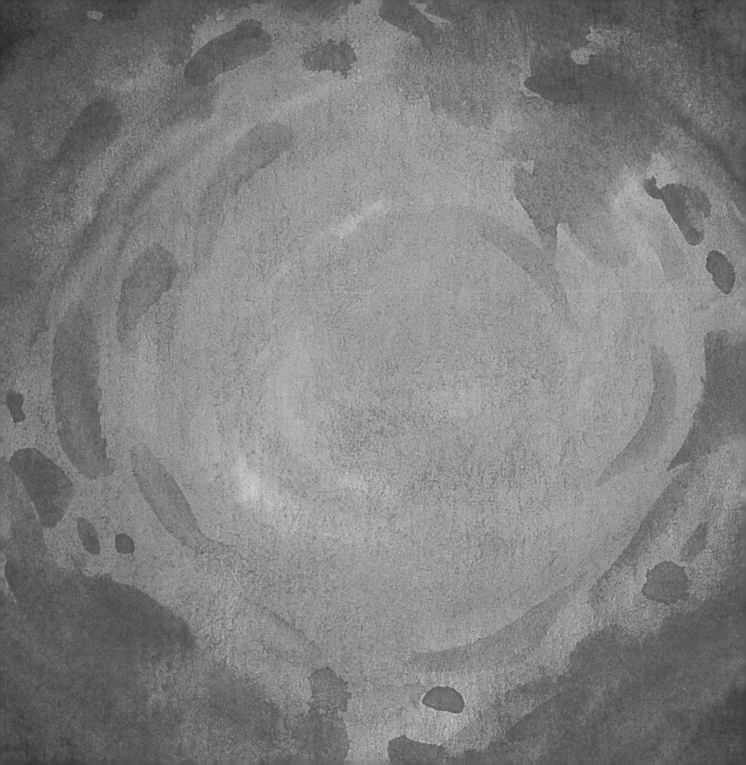

I AM YOGA

BY SUSAN VERDE · ART BY PETER H. REYNOLDS

Abrams Books for Young Readers · New York

The illustrations in this book were created using ink, gouache, watercolor, and tea.

Library of Congress Cataloging-in-Publication Data

Verde, Susan.
I am yoga / by Susan Verde ; illustrated by Peter H. Reynolds.
pages cm
Summary: As a young girl practices various standard yoga poses, she imagines herself as a tree touching the sky, a playful dog, a warrior, and more while relaxing and seeing how she fits into the world.
ISBN 978-1-4197-1664-5
[1. Yoga—Fiction. 2. Imagination—Fiction.]
I. Reynolds, Peter H., illustrator. II. Title.
PZ7.1.V46Iaah 2015
[E]—dc23
2014040993

Text copyright © 2015 Susan Verde
Illustrations copyright © 2015 Peter H. Reynolds
Book design by Chad W. Beckerman

Printed and bound in U.S.A.
20 19 18 17 16 15 14 13 12

Abrams Books for Young Readers are available at special discounts when purchased in quantity for premiums and promotions as well as fundraising or educational use. Special editions can also be created to specification. For details, contact specialsales@abramsbooks.com or the address below.

ABRAMS The Art of Books
195 Broadway, New York, NY 10007
abramsbooks.com

to Jennifer Cohen Harper, my beautiful friend
and mentor, and to yogis big and small
— S.V.

to Bruce and Carole Hart
— P.H.R.

When I feel
small
in a world
so big,

when I wonder how I fit in,

when the world is spinning so fast...

I tell my wiggling body:
be still.

I tell my
racing breath:
be
slow.

I close my eyes
and make room
in my mind,
in my heart,
to create and
imagine.

I can touch the sky.
I am so tall.

I can soar among the clouds.
I am so free.

I can sparkle with the stars.
I shimmer and shine.

I can dance with the moon.
I light up the night.

I can sail on the sea.
I go with the flow.

I can open my heart.
I feel love.

I can see far and wide.
I am focused.

I can turn things upside down.
I am playful.

I can stand up for me,

I can stand up for others,

I can stand up for peace.

I can open like a flower.
I am beautiful.

I can carry beauty with me.
I am full.

I can say I've had enough for today.
I relax.

I can rest.
I am calm.

Now the world is just
the right speed.
Now my world is just
the right size.

Now I see,
I fit in just fine.
I am Yoga. I can be anything!

Author's Note

The word "yoga" means union. Yoga is the connection between mind and body. My own yoga practice is a way to handle stress, find calm in my mind and strength in my body, and be present as an educator, a parent, a kid's yoga teacher, and a person in a busy world.

Kids *are* yoga. Their practice begins naturally as part of their development when they are just infants. Tummy time is Cobra pose. When they are on their backs grabbing for their toes, it is Happy Baby pose. As they grow, children, like adults, encounter stress on many levels, from bad dreams to arguments with siblings to pressure from friends. There's school-related stress, stress from overscheduling, and, in extreme cases, stress from trauma. The poses and games, the meditations and mindfulness activities of children's yoga help kids strengthen their bodies, calm their minds, and become aware of the mind-body connection in a noncompetitive, playful way. Kid's yoga, with all its components, is a toolbox for helping a person manage a world that often feels too big to handle.

My hope is that this playful story of what it means to *be* yoga serves as a way for children to tap into all that yoga has to offer. As they read, play, imagine, explore, express themselves, and breathe, they can know that whoever they are, however they are in this big world, they fit in just fine.

The Poses

Here is a list of the poses that are referred to in *I Am Yoga* as well as their Sanskrit names (where applicable) and a few notes on instruction. When teaching kids to breathe in yoga, we practice inhaling and exhaling slowly and deeply through the nose to calm the nervous system.

Mountain Pose (Tadasana):
Stand tall, with your feet together or slightly apart. Find an equal balance on both feet. Firm your thighs and pull in your belly. Roll your shoulders back and down away from your ears. You can let your arms hang down by your sides, palms facing forward, or lift them straight above your head and bring your palms together. You are a mountain.

Breathe in and out slowly. If you like, close your eyes and imagine you are strong and sturdy, still and calm.

Tree Pose (Vrksasana):
Before getting into this pose, find an unmoving spot on the floor or something directly in front of you to stare at to help you balance.

Begin in Mountain pose. From your mountain, lift your arms and reach out to either side, like the branches of a tree, to help you balance. Lift one foot, turning your knee out to the side, and place your foot either below the knee of the standing leg or above it. Breathing slowly in and out, bring your arms up over your head and imagine yourself growing like a tree. Slowly lower your hands to your chest, place your foot down, and repeat on the other side.

Airplane Pose (Virabhadrasana III):
Begin in Mountain pose. Reach your arms out to either side. Breathe in. Upon breathing out, lean forward and lift and extend one leg behind you. Hold the pose for a few breaths. Lower the lifted leg and repeat on the other side.

Star Pose (Utthita Tadasana):
Stand with your feet wide apart. Stretch your arms out to either side. Breathe in deeply and twinkle and shine with every breath.

Half Moon Pose (Ardha Chandrasana):

Start in Mountain pose. Bend forward and place your right hand on the ground about a hand's length away from and slightly to the outside of your right foot. Lift your left leg parallel to the floor. Once you feel balanced, lift your left arm and reach for the sky. Breathe deeply. Look straight ahead or up at your hand. Open your body, imagining you are leaning back against a wall and expanding your chest. Put everything back on the ground and repeat on the other side.

Boat Pose (Navasana):

Sit on the floor with your knees bent and feet together on the ground. Reach your arms out in front of you on either side of your knees. Balancing on your bottom, lift your toes off the ground; when you feel ready, you can either straighten your legs out in front of you or keep your knees bent. Try keeping your legs in the air while singing "Row, Row, Row Your Boat."

Camel Pose (Ustrasana):

Kneel on the floor with your toes curled under you or the tops of your feet flat against the ground. Sit on your shins and reach back for your heels. Lift your heart to the sky, imagining the shape of a camel's hump. Another option is to stand on your shins and support your lower back with your hands, drawing your shoulders together and lifting your heart to the sky.

Eagle Pose (Garudasana):

Stand in Mountain pose. Bend your left leg and cross your right leg over the left. Lift your left arm in front of you, bending at the elbow, and circle your right arm underneath your left, turning your hands so your palms meet, or just bring your forearms together from elbows to fingertips.

Find balance first, then slowly lower your hips, as if sitting in a chair. Breathe in and out slowly, as if you are an eagle watching something far below. Unwrap your arms and spread your wings as you come out of the pose. Repeat on the opposite side.

Downward Dog Pose (Adho Mukha Svanasana):

Start on your hands and knees, with your toes curled under. Breathe in, and, as you breathe out, lift your hips in the air, straightening your legs and pressing your heels toward the floor. Push your palms into the floor, with your fingertips facing forward. Look between your knees. Wag your tail, bark, lift one leg or the other. Be playful!

Warrior Poses:

The warrior poses are meant to make you feel strong and powerful with the understanding that you don't need anger or aggression to stand up for yourself and others. It's a great opportunity to talk about when one might need to be a warrior, referencing peaceful warriors in history (e.g., Martin Luther King Jr., Gandhi). Try saying something positive about yourself out loud in each pose. For example, "I am strong!" "I am peaceful!" or "I am brave!"

Warrior I (Virabhadrasana I):

Start in Mountain pose. Step your right foot back, with your toes pointing slightly out to the side and keeping your right leg straight. Bend your left leg so your knee falls over your ankle. Face your torso forward, raise your arms over your head, and reach for the sky. Hold for a few breaths. Return to Mountain pose and repeat on the other side.

Warrior II (Virabhadrasana II):

From Warrior I pose, with your left foot forward and your right foot in the back and out to the side, reach your left arm straight forward and your right arm backward, so they both are parallel with the ground, with your torso facing to the right. Reach out through your fingertips and turn your head to look out over your left hand. Repeat on the other side.

Peaceful Warrior (Shanti Virabhadrasana):

From Warrior II, with your left foot in front and right leg in the back and to the side, arch backward, letting your left hand reach for the sky behind your head. Your right arm can rest on your back leg. Repeat on the other side.

Flower Pose:

Sit on the ground and bring the soles of your feet together. Dive your hands in between your knees and out and under your legs. Lift your feet off the ground, knees pointing out to the side, and balance in your flower. Your feet will most likely separate in the air. Breathe in and out slowly. What kind of flower are you?

Bow/Basket Pose (Dhanurasana):

Start flat on your belly, with your hands alongside your body, palms facing up. Bend your knees and reach each arm back, taking hold of the outside of each shin, ankle, or foot. Breathe in and reach your heels toward the sky, lifting your heart and your thighs off the floor. Breathe in and out while holding this position and looking straight ahead. You may find yourself rocking back and forth as you breathe. What's in your basket? When you are ready, release your body gently to the floor.

Child's Pose (Balasana):

Start by kneeling on the floor, with the tops of your feet resting on the ground, big toes touching. Sit back on your heels, either keeping your knees together or separating them the width of your hips. Bring your head down gently to the floor in front of you. Your hands can stay by your side or you can reach them out in front of you. Breathe in and out and hold the pose as long as it is comfortable. Use this pose as a chance to relax and rest.

Relaxation Pose (Savasana):

Lie down on your back with your legs straight and your arms by your sides, palms facing up. Let your legs separate naturally and your feet flop out to the side. Try not to talk or look around. If you are comfortable, close your eyes. Let every part of your body relax and sink into the ground and be supported by the earth underneath you.

Relaxation pose can be a challenging pose for kids. There are many techniques to help children clear their minds and relax their bodies while holding this pose—for example, placing a small object on the belly and focusing on that object as they breathe deeply, remaining still.

This is the final pose in all yoga practices. Feel proud of and thankful for all poses you have been able to practice.

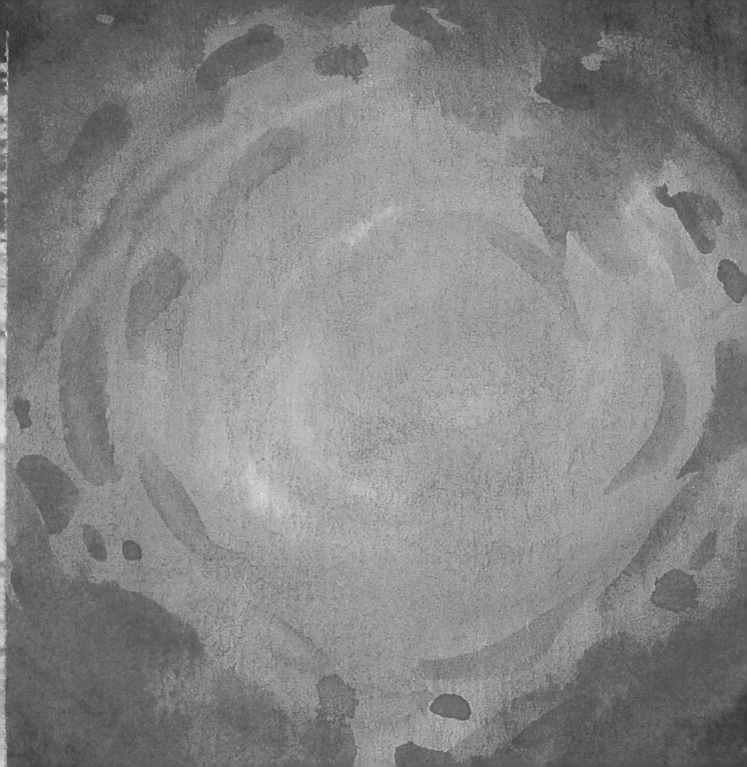